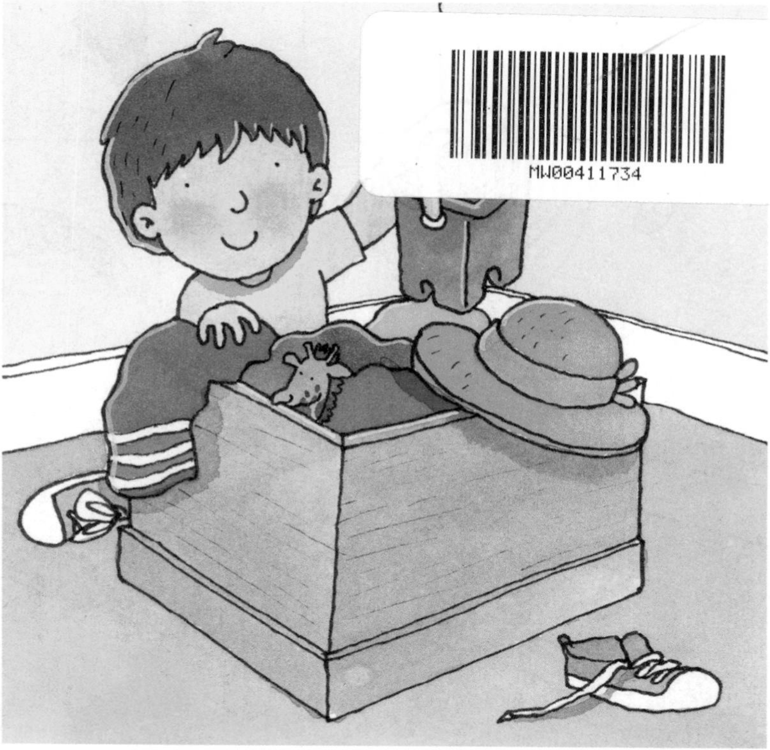

Find the pail.

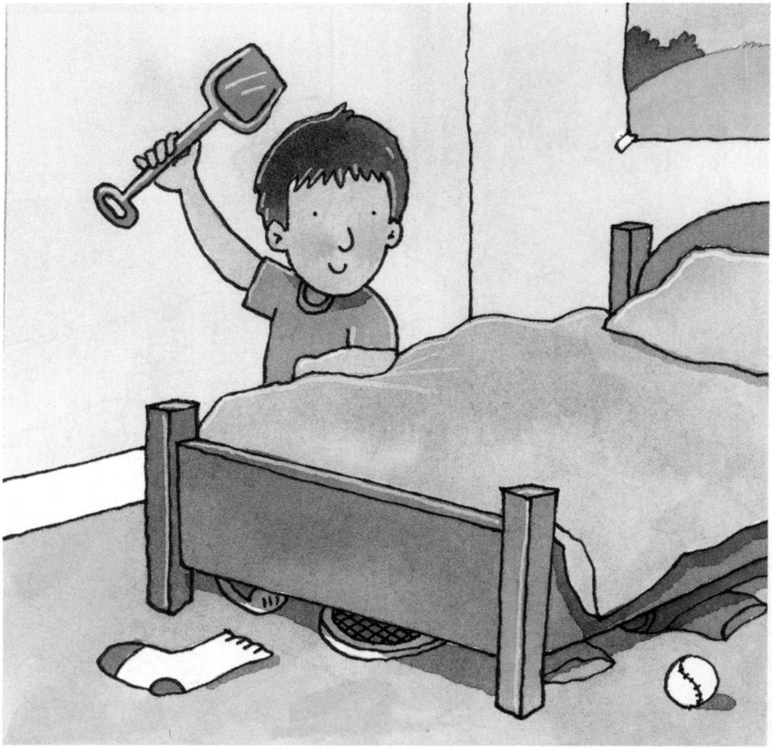

Find the shovel.

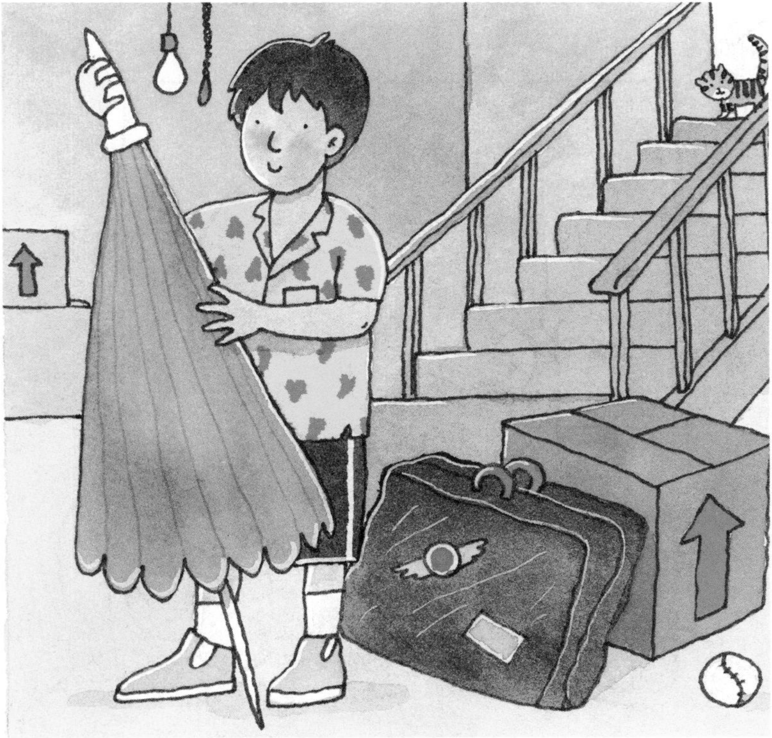

Find the umbrella.

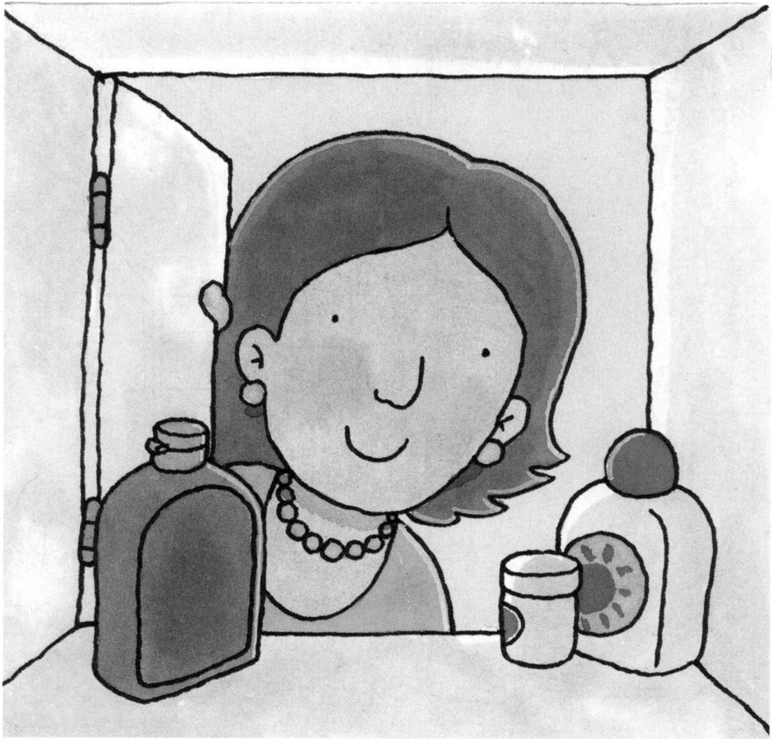

Find the lotion.

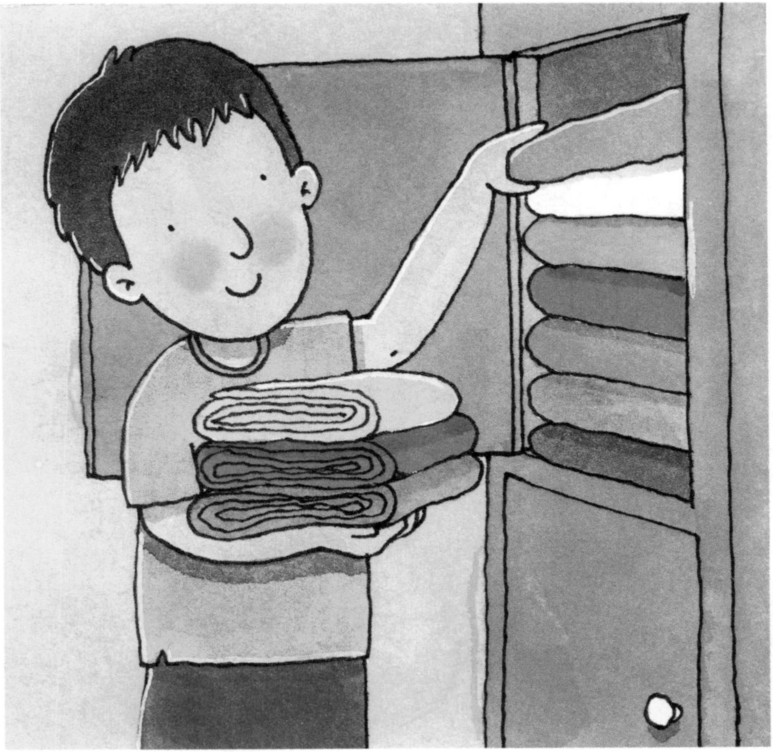

Find the towels.

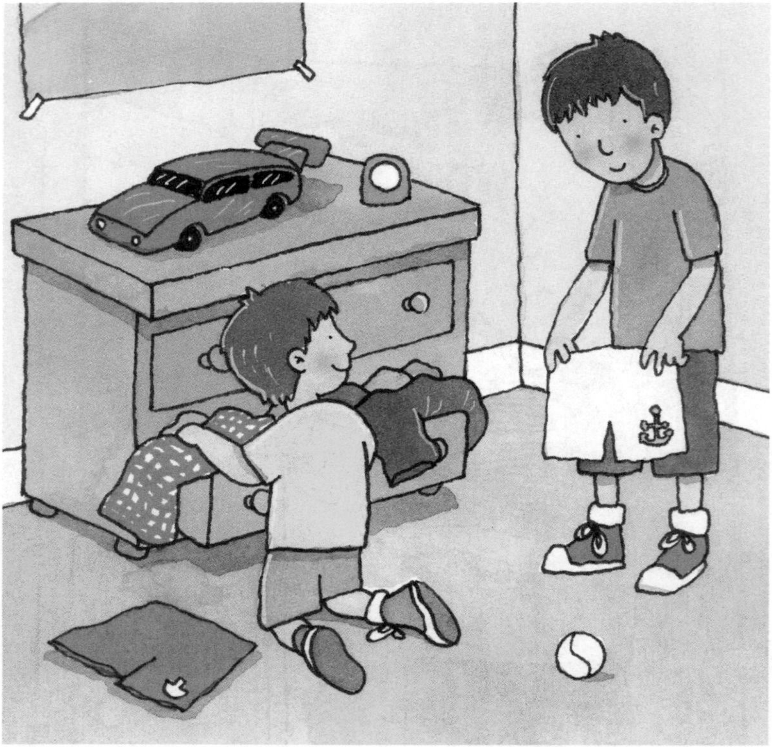

Find the suits.

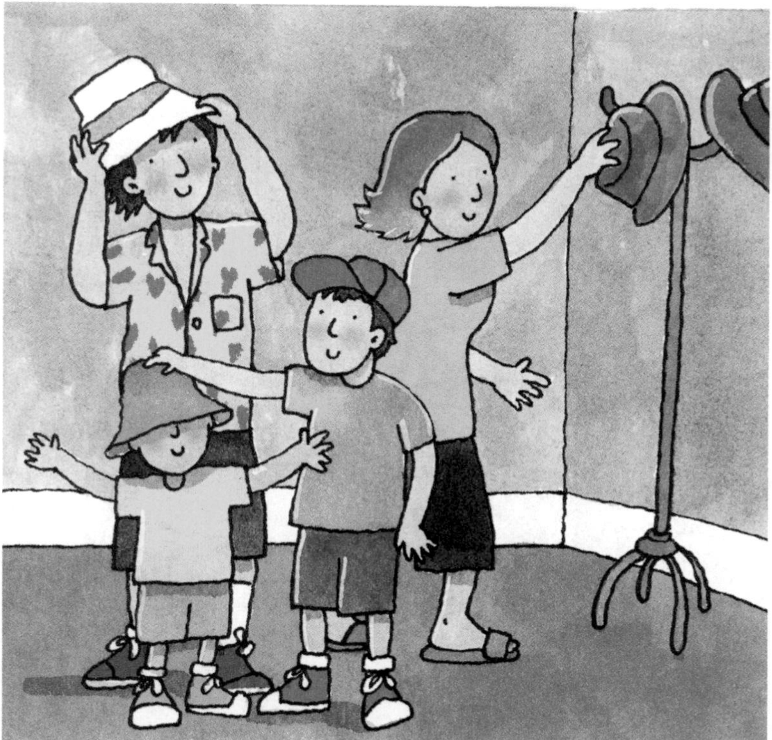

Find the hats.

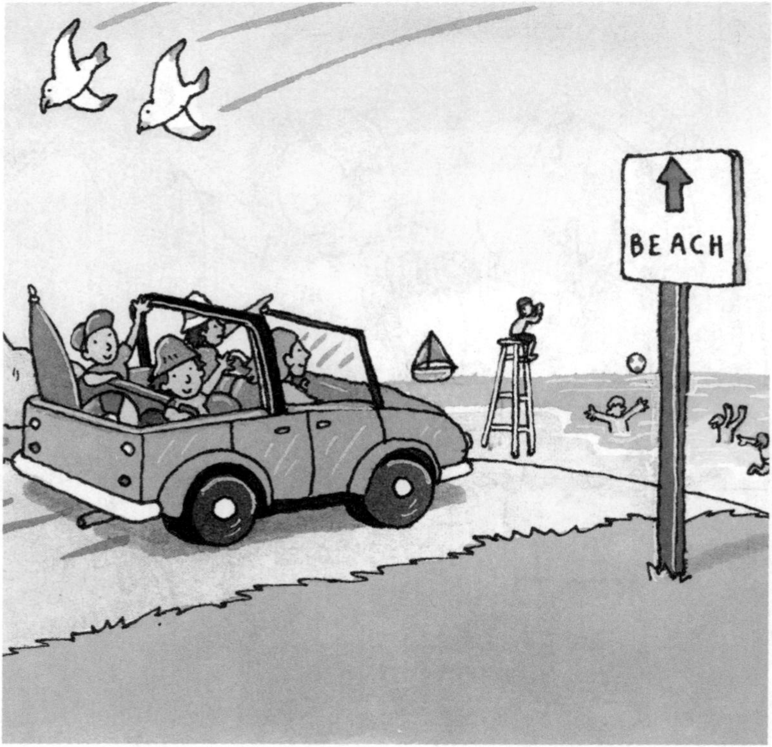

Find the beach!